BEASTS
—OF—
OLYMPUS

GROSSET & DUNLAP
Published by the Penguin Group
Penguin Group (USA) LLC, 375 Hudson Street, New York, New York 10014, USA

USA | Canada | UK | Ireland | Australia | New Zealand | India | South Africa | China

penguin.com
A Penguin Random House Company

Library of Congress Cataloging-in-Publication Data is available.

ISBN 978-0-448-46194-6   10 9 8 7 6 5 4 3 2 1

BEASTS
—OF—
OLYMPUS

by Lucy Coats   art by Brett Bean

Hound of Hades

GROSSET & DUNLAP
An Imprint of Penguin Group (USA) LLC

CHAPTER 1

OFFICIAL STABLE BOY
TO THE GODS

Demon, son of the god Pan, and brand-new
Official Stable Boy to the gods, had a bellyache.

It was a bellyache of monumental proportions.
Even Atlas, the giant Titan, had never had a
bellyache as big as this one, Demon decided.

He lay under his blanket in the loft above the
Stables and wished he hadn't eaten those final
ten honey cakes that the goddess Hestia had
offered him as "a going-home snack." He was still
so full after the gods' celebration feast that he

hadn't slept a wink all night. The prospect of his usual early-morning task of shoveling barrowsful of poo down to the hundred-armed monsters in Tartarus was making him feel greener than moldy spinach. He groaned and turned over on his straw mattress, closing his eyes and wishing that Eos, the dawn goddess, would hold off on opening up the day.

"Hey! Demon! I'm hungry! Where's my breakfast?" came a loud shout from below. There was a scrape and clatter of claws on the ladder as the griffin popped its head through the trapdoor. It leaned over and poked its sharp beak into Demon's stomach.

"Go 'way, griffin," Demon moaned. "I'm ill. Very ill. In fact, I may die any minute."

"Huh!" said the griffin. "Well, I wouldn't lie around being ill and dying for too long. I hear from the nymphs that you're going to have an

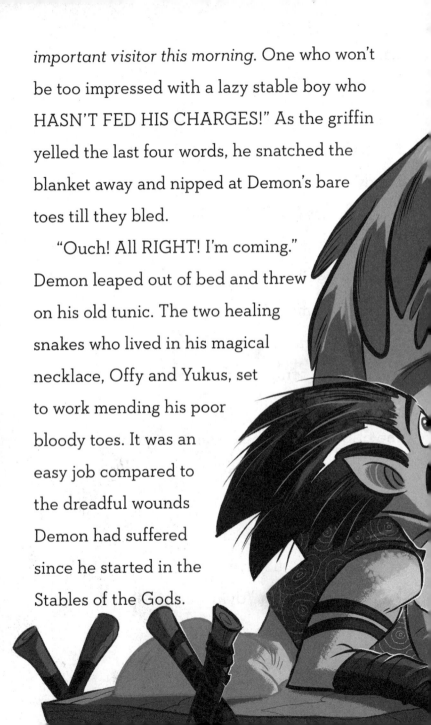

important visitor this morning. One who won't be too impressed with a lazy stable boy who HASN'T FED HIS CHARGES!" As the griffin yelled the last four words, he snatched the blanket away and nipped at Demon's bare toes till they bled.

"Ouch! All RIGHT! I'm coming." Demon leaped out of bed and threw on his old tunic. The two healing snakes who lived in his magical necklace, Offy and Yukus, set to work mending his poor bloody toes. It was an easy job compared to the dreadful wounds Demon had suffered since he started in the Stables of the Gods.

The magic snakes were soon done and slithered back up around his neck. "What important visitor?" he asked the griffin as he tied his silver rope belt around his waist.

"Aha!" said the griffin mysteriously, tapping one grubby claw against its beak.

"You are a very annoying creature sometimes," said Demon. "Anyway, I don't have time to worry about some stupid visitor. As you so kindly reminded me just now, I've got work to do." But as he descended the ladder, a small nervous lump lodged itself in his chest somewhere just above his solar plexus. What if the important visitor was Hera? What if she had another impossible task for him to do? What if she threatened to turn him into a heap of charcoal? He could hear the griffin giggling to itself above him. That was never good news.

Demon headed off to clear out the muck

created by the Cattle of the Sun, make sure
the nymphs had milked the unicorns, and
feed leftover ambrosia cake to all the immortal
creatures. By the time he finished, he had a
pounding headache, and his stomach felt like a
herd of man-eating horses was galloping around
in it. Luckily his new friend, the nine-headed
Hydra, had helped him out by carrying buckets,
rakes, mops, and brooms for him in all its mouths.
It also pushed the poo wheelbarrow with its tail.

"Thanks, Doris," he said as he tipped the
last of the stinky mess down the poo chute. The
monsters who lived below roared appreciatively.
The Hydra grinned at him, its hundreds of sharp
teeth glinting in the pale sunlight reflecting off
Eos's pink fluffy bedsheets, hanging out to dry
in the dawn sky. It loved having a proper name,
and it was so grateful to Demon for saving its life
that it would do almost anything for him.

"Doris likes helping," it said. Then it fluttered its eighteen pairs of long green eyelashes at Demon. "Snackies for Doris now?" it asked hopefully.

Demon tossed it a few bits of leftover ambrosia cake, and Doris retired to a corner of the Stables to chew on them. There was soon a spreading pool of drool beneath it—Hydras were messy eaters at the best of times. Demon headed over to the hospital shed to see if Hephaestus's magical medicine box would have something that would make his stomach feel better. It was meant for the beasts, really, but at this point he didn't care. He just wanted to feel normal again. As he opened the door to the shed, the comforting smell of aloe- and lavender-soaked bandages wafted out to greet him. The big square silver box lay on the table in front of him. As he lifted the lid, the familiar soft blue symbols sprang to life.

"State the nature of your beast's emergency medical problem," the box said in its metallic voice.

"It's not a beast. It's me," said Demon, rubbing his poor stomach and feeling very sorry for himself all over again. "I've got a horrible bellyache and a thumping headache, and I think I might die if you don't do something about it." He didn't say that the bellyache was from eating too many of Hestia's honey cakes.

A long silver tentacle with a flat disk on the end of it shot out of the box and snaked down the front of Demon's tunic. It was cold and made him jump. After a few seconds it retreated back the way it had come. "Error code 435. Human ailment. Does not compute with data program. Unable to assist. Thank you for your inquiry." The box closed abruptly, with a final, resounding click.

"Stupid box," said Demon, kicking the table so it rattled. The box opened a tiny bit, and a pointed silver tongue stuck out in Demon's direction.

It made a very rude farting noise, then the box snapped shut again.

As Demon stormed out of the hospital shed, slamming the door behind him, he saw a swirling cloud of utter darkness burst out of a large crack in the ground. He was sure the crack hadn't been there five minutes before. The cloud raced toward the Stables at an alarming speed with a sound like a thousand hammers pounding. Demon's heart began to thump. This must be the griffin's Important Visitor arriving.

CHAPTER 2
THE IMPORTANT VISITOR

Demon reached the double doors of the Stables just before the thundering cloud of darkness did. He straightened his tunic hurriedly and ran his fingers through his hair, hoping there wasn't straw in it. A large, pointy-booted foot emerged from the inky murk. Demon caught a whiff of something strange. It smelled sort of damp and musty, like old, dead things mixed with the scent of burning hair. The foot was followed by a tall figure, cloaked all in black. In one gloved hand it carried a huge helmet, studded with bloodred rubies, and in the other a set of reins, which it tossed to Demon. The reins appeared to be attached to something (or somethings) within the blackness.

"Hurry up and ssstable those for me, dear boy," the figure said, its sibilant voice soft and dangerous. "And find them sssome meat, will you? That ussselesss sssatyr Sssilenusss tried to feed them leftover ambrosia cake lassst time I was here. They burned all the hair off his legs, as I recall." With that, the figure strode off toward Zeus and Hera's palace, leaving Demon staring openmouthed after it.

"He arrived then, I see," said the griffin into Demon's left ear, nearly making him drop his set of reins.

"Wh-who . . . wh-what . . . ?" he stammered. "Er, I mean . . . who IS he?" asked Demon, finally managing to get his words out properly.

"That? Oh, that's Hades. Lord of the Underworld. Terror of Tartarus. God of death. Bit overwhelming, isn't he?" said the griffin. Then it sniffed. "I see he's brought those wretched things with him again," it remarked sourly. "His pride and joy, they are, but I wish he'd stick to horses. Better put them in the fireproof pens at the end. They nearly torched the place when they were here before. And as for what they did to poor old Silenus . . . it doesn't bear thinking about. He had blisters for months."

Demon gave an experimental tug on the reins Hades had thrown him. They seemed to be made of some kind of pliable blue-black metal, light but very strong. Whatever was at the other end roared and tugged back, and two huge jets of blue-white flame lanced out of the darkness straight at him. He and the griffin ducked and rolled out of the way just in time as five bales of the Cattle of the Sun's special hay frizzled into nothingness behind them.

"Play them your dad's pipes, quick!" yelled the griffin through the roaring. "Don't know if they work on earth dragons, but it's worth a try!" It scuttled around the corner of the Stables and disappeared. Demon hung on to the lashing, thrashing reins with one hand, while fumbling in the pocket of his tunic with the other. *Dragons?* he thought. *Dragons? DRAGONS?* His legs wanted to run one way and his frantically beating heart the other. He wrenched the Pan pipes out of his pocket, swung them to his lips with one swift movement, and started to blow. The cascade of tinkling notes dropped into the roaring flame, and immediately the reins fell limp in Demon's other hand. A crooning noise came from the darkness, and two vast scaly bronze heads slowly emerged out of the gloom. Their huge eyes were as big as Hera's golden dinner plates, and deep purple fires burned in their depths as the beasts walked forward. Their enormous taloned feet shook the ground at every step. Sharp spikes covered their bodies in unassailable armor, and drifts of ghostly pale smoke hung from their nostrils.

Demon blew the pipes for all he was worth, not daring to stop as he tugged the vast beasts toward the rock-walled pens at the very back of the Stables. He'd always wondered what creatures they were for. Now he knew.

If he'd thought getting dragons into their pen was hard work, unharnessing sleepy ones with one hand was almost impossible. He managed it eventually, using the spikes as a ladder, then throwing the undone metal straps outside the dragon pens for polishing. When he had finished, Demon walked out backward, slammed the fireproof gates behind him, and ran a safe distance before he plucked up the courage to stop playing.

There was a sudden blissful silence. Not a beast in the Stables was moving or making a noise. When he peeked into the griffin's cage, it was asleep on the floor, whiffling gently through its beak. All his other charges were the same. Even the giant scorpion was lying down on its back with its stinger curled up. Demon grinned, looking at his trusty Pan pipes.

"Thanks, Dad," he whispered. His bellyache had gone now, and his head felt clear. He'd survived. Again. But then he remembered the other thing Hades had asked him to do. "Meat. Where do I find meat?" he wondered. All there usually was to eat on Olympus was ambrosia cake. Except on feast days.

Feast days! That was it! Maybe there was some meat left over from last night's feast. He definitely remembered seeing some roasted ribs going past on Hephaestus's magical serving carts. He shoved his pipes into his pocket again and set out for the forge under the mountain. The smith god always gave him good advice.

Hephaestus was lying down on a rocky couch with a grimy blanket over him and a stained handkerchief spread over his head. One of his silvery-gold robot automatons was pumping the forge bellows gently, keeping the fire to a muted glow. It raised a metal finger to its lips.

"Sh!" it said. Hephaestus's robots never used two words where one short one would do.

Demon looked at the god of the forge. Was it worth the risk of waking him? Heffy wasn't the sort to turn a boy into charcoal, but you never knew with the gods. They could get nasty in a minute. Still, given the choice between Hades or Hephaestus being angry with him, he'd take his chances with Heffy any day. Demon drew in a deep breath and tiptoed over to the couch, ignoring the robot's attempts to hush him.

He coughed quietly; then, as there was no response from the sleeping god, a little louder. Still nothing. One grubby, charcoal-dusted finger poked out from under the blanket, so Demon bent down and tugged at it gently.

"Ahem! Hephaestus! Sir! Your Godishness! I wouldn't wake you, only it's a bit of an emergency . . ."

There was a snorting and a harrumphing from under the handkerchief, with a few indistinguishable words thrown in between. "Wassermatter . . . *snortle* . . . thoughtIsaidnovisitors . . . *harrumph* . . . owmyheadhurts . . . !"

Demon bent down and looked at the groaning god sympathetically. He knew just how Heffy felt. Just then Hephaestus sat up unexpectedly, beard all wild and snarly, eyes red-rimmed and half shut. His head met Demon's with a clash. Demon tumbled backward and into the robot, who fell over with a metallic crashing sound.

"AARRRGGHH!" roared the god, leaping up and dancing around the forge, head in his enormous hands.

"OOOF!" said Demon, a heavy metal foot clipping his shoulder as little bright stars of pain flared around his forehead.

"I THOUGHT I GAVE ORDERS THAT I WAS NOT TO BE AWAKENED!" Hephaestus shouted, sparks flying from his eyes and the tips of his fingers. The robot said nothing. It was too busy collecting pieces of itself and reattaching them.

"I'm veryveryvery sorry, it was all m-m-my fault," said Demon in a very small, shaky voice. He'd rarely seen Hephaestus angry before, and he wasn't sure he wanted to again. The god was batting at his beard, which was now on fire from the sparks that had landed in it.

"Zeus-blasted stable boy," said Hephaestus in slightly milder tones. "What's so Hades-bebothered important that you have to wake a god from his richly deserved beauty sleep?"

"Well," said Demon, "since you mention Hades . . ." He explained about earth dragons

needing meat, not ambrosia cake. "I don't want to get my legs burned off like poor Silenus did," he finished. "I don't think even Offy and Yukus could mend that."

Hephaestus stood there for a moment, pulling out clumps of singed beard and scratching his head while he thought.

"Hestia," he said finally. "She usually supervises cleanup after a feast. If there's any meat about, she'll know where it's kept. You can find her in the kitchens." He looked around. "Where's that wretched robot when you need it?" The robot stepped out from behind a pillar. "Here, you—take Demon to the kitchens. And put that arm on the right way 'round before you come back." He limped over to his couch and lay down again, sighing loudly. "Now go away and leave me to my headache."

CHAPTER 3

THE KITCHENS OF THE GODS

The robot led Demon through the winding back ways of Olympus and past places he'd never seen before. He hadn't realized that palaces had back doors with garbage outside them, nor that the gods and goddesses would need normal things like clotheslines. He ducked under a row of fragrant yellow spider-silk robes hung out to dry in the morning breeze. They smelled like soft sunshine and sweet flower petals as he brushed against them. Demon wanted to stop and look around, but the robot was setting a good pace with its long metal legs. Besides, he knew he had to find the meat for the earth dragons before Hades came back.

A little farther along, as they turned in to a white marble courtyard, a delicious aroma hit him square in the nose. It was both familiar and unfamiliar at the same time. "Mmm," he said, sniffing with his eyes half closed. What *was* that? It smelled good. Suddenly his stomach rumbled loudly. He didn't see how he could be hungry again after last night, but it appeared his stomach had different ideas.

"Kitchens," said the robot, pointing to an open wooden door. Demon thanked it, and it turned without another word and took off. He went up to the door and put his head around it, peering in. Inside was a pantry, with hundreds of dirty gold and silver dishes on every surface.

Almost as many jeweled goblets were piled up in heaps on the floor.

There seemed to be nobody around, so Demon picked his way through the chaos and went in. This was where the delicious smell was coming from. He saw a huge kitchen, bustling with activity. There were small cooking fires burning everywhere. Their light reflected off the gleaming sides of a thousand copper pots, jugs, and whole racks full of shining silver knives. Around the sides of the kitchen stood a series of long tables where nymphs were chopping and pouring and mixing. The air was full of the sound of sizzling. In the middle of it all stood the goddess Hestia. She held a large wooden spoon in her hand and directed the whole frantic cooking operation. She was wearing the same apron embroidered with pots and pans he'd seen her wearing when he visited her palace

to get some eternal flame to cure the Cretan
Bull's bovine pentagastric marine pyrosaturitis.
Close by her, several fauns were wearing smaller
aprons. They were working hard at frying large
amounts of sizzling meat in enormous pans.
Others were scurrying around, pulling trays of
steaming bread out of huge ovens. One very
small faun was standing on a stool beside Hestia,
fanning her face with a large palm leaf. It was
very, very hot.

"Ah! Our Official Beast
Keeper has arrived,"
said Hestia. "Hello,
Pandemonius. Would you
like one of my special *loukaniko*
sausages for breakfast? They're
a brand-new recipe—I added
cinnamon and apples to the mix.

All the gods and goddesses always want a home-cooked breakfast when they wake up after drinking Dionysius's silly grape juice." As she spoke, she whisked a sausage out of the nearest pan, grabbed a hot roll, slapped the meat into it, and handed it to Demon. The smell was divine. He bit into it, not caring that it was piping hot. It was utterly delicious, sweet and spicy and full of just the right amount of meat.

Oh no! Meat. He'd forgotten for a second.

"Yum!" he said hastily and indistinctly, chewing frantically. "Yum yum YUM!" He didn't want to hurry this. It would be back to horrid ambrosia cake soon. "Er, Your Goddessness, I was wondering . . ."

Hestia shoved another full roll into his free hand. "Try this one," she said. "It's got just a touch of pine nuts and wild thyme honey. Oh, and don't worry, I know what you've come for.

I saw Hades go storming past about half an hour ago. I suppose he was upset about missing the feast last night. Glaukos over there is already loading up some supplies for those wretched dragons of his." She pointed to a faun throwing large pieces of cooked flesh into a battered silver wheelbarrow.

Demon felt like falling to his knees with gratitude. Hestia was definitely the nicest goddess ever.

"Fank you," he mumbled around another mouthful of bread and sausage. Hestia just waved him toward the wheelbarrow, before turning to smack a nearby faun about the horns with her wooden spoon. There was black smoke coming out of the frying pan he was looking after.

"Use those tongs!" she yelled. "Did I say I wanted them burned to a crisp? I'll burn *you* to a crisp if you don't CONCENTRATE!" Demon hurried away. Hestia might be nice, but he wasn't taking any risks.

All the beasts were still asleep when Demon got back to the Stables, panting slightly from pushing the heavy barrowful of meat. He tiptoed up to the rock-walled pen and unlocked the fireproof doors, Pan pipes at the ready just in case. But both dragons were slumped on the floor. Small streams of ghostly smoke rose from their cavernous nostrils as they snored. He quickly tossed the meat into the large stone trough gouged out of the wall, hoping they wouldn't wake. He didn't want to be in the same place as two hungry dragons. They might see him as a tasty snack to finish off their meal. Sure enough, just as he was fastening the doors, there was a flash of flame and a great roaring and chomping noise. Obviously, like most beasts, dragons woke up at the smell of food.

He felt a sharp claw dig into his shoulder. "Saved me some meat, did you, Pan's scrawny kid?"

asked the griffin menacingly. "You'd better have." Clearly the dragons were not the only ones to have been woken up by the smell of food. Luckily there were a couple of small legs of lamb left. Demon tossed them to the beast, who caught them in his huge curved beak.

"Eat them quietly," he hissed at the creature. "Or they'll all want some." Most of the beasts survived on stale ambrosia cake. The more carnivorous ones complained about it dreadfully. He picked up the dragon harness and struggled to sling it over his shoulder. Although his muscles had become stronger with all the shoveling and brushing and barrowing of poo he had to do daily, the mess of metal straps and breastplates was very heavy. He hauled them out to the front of the Stables and sat down on a bale of golden hay. Using a bottle of Eternal All-Shine he'd gotten from Melanie the naiad, he began to clean and polish the disgusting, charcoal-crusted harnesses.

Twenty minutes later, the harnesses were shining like new, all ready for Hades's return. Demon just hoped he'd done a good enough job not to be turned into toast.

It seemed that he didn't have long to wait for the god of death. Just as he'd finished clearing away the clean white bones that were all the griffin had left of its meal, the bars of sunlight falling across the floor of the Stables faded and turned to gray. There was a sudden breath of must and mold in the darkening air. Before Demon could even turn around, a heavy hand fell on his shoulder.

"Ssso, ssstable boy," said Hades in his soft, hissing voice. "I sssee you haven't been eaten by my dragonsss. Yet." There was a sinister pause, and then he went on, his fingers digging in a bit, so Demon could feel the prick of his long nails. "My sssissster Hera tellsss me you're good at mending sssick beastsss. Are you?"

Demon didn't quite know what to say. If he said yes, it might sound like boasting, which he knew the gods didn't like.

"Well, Your M-m-mighty D-d-dark Goddishness, I wouldn't say *good*, exactly. I've had a lot of help from my father and Hephaestus . . . a-and a bit of good fortune with my cures." He kept his eyes firmly on the floor, hoping that Hades would just go away and leave him alone now that he'd answered. But no such luck. The god clapped him on the shoulder so hard that Demon fell to his knees.

"A modessst boy. I like that. You'll need to pack up your medical thingsss, ssstable boy. I need you in the Underworld for a while. I have a sssickly hound who needsss your attention urgently. Now, take me to my dragonsss. I have sssome treatsss for them." As Demon led Hades toward the dragon pens, his mind was whirling. How could he go down to the Underworld? Surely that was just for dead people. And who would look after the Stables if he was gone? He left Hades crooning to his dragons as if they were puppies, tossing strings of entrails into the air for them to catch. Then Demon took to his heels and ran as fast as he could to the hospital shed. As soon as he was inside, he scooped up some lavender and aloe bandages, which he stuffed inside his tunic, and grabbed his magical silver medicine box by one handle. The griffin poked its head through the doorway.

"Bad luck, Pan's scrawny kid. Word is you've got to go downstairs and visit with the Lord of Hell. I'd pack your warm cloak. Gets chilly down there, so I hear." Demon set off back to the Stables, the griffin loping beside him on its lion paws. Demon lugged the box behind him, bumping it over the rough earth as he ran. It let out an indignant squawk, and four short legs appeared at its bottom corners.

"Emergency locomotion program in progress," it squawked.

"Did I know you could do that?" Demon said, stopping dead in his surprise and letting go of the handle. The box bumped into him, knocking him over. "Ouch!" he said. His knees were going to be permanently scabbed at this rate.

"That box is full of surprises," said the griffin. "Heffy gave it some upgrades, remember? Now come on. Hurry up. You have dragons to harness, and it doesn't do to keep Hades waiting. Not the most patient of gods, old Hellface."

"But who's going to look after all of you?" Demon asked. "I'm supposed to be the Official

Beast Keeper to the gods, but how can I do my job properly if I keep getting taken away from Olympus by gods and goddesses?"

"Don't worry about that," said the griffin. "Doris will do cleanup if you offer it snackies of extra ambrosia. Beats me why it likes that disgusting stuff," it added gloomily.

A short time later, Demon had given Doris the Hydra enough extra ambrosia cake to keep it happy for days. It had given him loving licks with nine slimy green tongues and promised to keep the Stables clean till he returned. After that, he wrestled the harness onto two well-fed, happy dragons. He then led them up to the swirl of impenetrable black mist where Hades was waiting, tapping one pointy black boot impatiently. The box followed closely at his heels like a faithful dog.

"Hitch them up, ssstable boy, hitch them up,"

said the god of death. So Demon closed his eyes, tugged on the reins, and stepped forward into the darkness. As soon as the mist touched him, it felt like he was being sucked down into a pit of grief. All the sad things that had ever happened in his life swirled through his head at once. The time the baby chicks had fallen into the pond and drowned. The time he hadn't been able to save his favorite pet hen from the foxes. The time he'd found a wolf cub in a hunter's trap. His mother weeping over a patient she hadn't been able to save . . . He stood, frozen, the blue-black metal reins dropping unnoticed from his hand, tears pouring down his cheeks.

"Ah," said Hades. "I'd forgotten about the wretched ssside effect my pretty missst has on anyone who isn't me. Here, boy, put thisss on and don't lose it. You'll need it down below. And for Hermesss'sss sssake, wipe your nose.

I don't want boogersss sssmeared all over my niccce chariot." His gloved hand held out a ring made of shiny black stone. Demon fumbled it onto his middle finger, where it settled, seeming to shrink and cling like a small band of cold fog. Immediately the feeling of sadness lifted, and as it did, he noticed a chariot in front of him. Fixed to the back of its blue-black metal frame were two red lights in the shape of eyes. As Demon stepped closer, they swiveled around to watch him. The dragons backed themselves between the shafts, and Demon buckled the straps to hold them in. He patted them on their scaly shoulders and turned to Hades.

"All ready, Your Fabulous Formidableness," Demon said, wiping his nose with the back of a grubby hand and sounding almost cheerful in his relief at not feeling sad anymore. The god shuddered slightly and held out a black handkerchief.

"Revolting boy," he said, climbing into the driving seat. Demon started to follow him in, but Hades held up one black-gloved hand. "Nuh-uh, ssstable boy! No one travels with me. I'll sssee you down in the Underworld sssoon. Mind the ghosssts on your way in from the gatesss." With a malevolent grin, he cracked a whip of blue lightning above the dragons' heads, and immediately they plunged downward into the opening that had just appeared at their feet.

Demon stood staring in shock as the red eye-lights of the chariot vanished, and the opening snapped shut again as if it had never been. Did Hades really expect him to get to the gates of the Underworld all on his own?

Apparently the answer was yes.

CHAPTER 4

JOURNEY TO THE UNDERWORLD

"Oh," said Demon finally, his mouth hanging open. "But . . ."

The griffin cackled behind him. "Expecting a lift, were you, Pan's scrawny kid? Nope. You'll have to do it the normal way—get Charon the Ferryman to row you across the Styx and all that. Remember to take a couple of coins for him—and a couple for the way back, if you're lucky enough to survive. Go on, hurry up and hop on the Iris Express. She'll take you where you need to go. He wasn't joking when he said 'ssseee you sssoon,' you know." The griffin's imitation of Hades's snakelike voice was uncannily accurate.

Demon trudged back to his room to fetch the coins and then headed to the Iris Express. He was still followed by the box, which was staying remarkably silent. He forgot all about his warm cloak in his worry about what to say to Iris. He'd never summoned the gods' messenger before.

"Er, Iris Express, please. For me and my box. To go to the gates of the Underworld," he said nervously. There was a whoosh and a swish, and a rainbow arced down from the blue sky and landed in front of him.

"Unaccompanied minors and inanimate objects must belt up," said a tinkly voice from just above the rainbow as Demon stepped on. Immediately, multicolored bands looped themselves around him and the box, pinning them both so they couldn't move. Demon's heart began to beat very fast, remembering his last trip on the Iris Express. He closed his eyes and gritted his teeth, waiting for it to plunge earthward.

"Hold on, Iris," said a light, cheerful voice. "Wait for me." Demon opened his eyes. Standing in front of him was a tall, thin god with a mischievous smile on his face. Under one arm he carried a silver helmet. He had a strange carved staff in his hand, around which two golden snakes looped and turned in an endless figure eight. Demon recognized Hermes, chief messenger of the gods, and stood up as straight as he could while being strapped in.

"Good morning, Your Gargantuan Godness," he said politely.

Hermes laughed. "Hello, Pandemonius. No

need for the flattery. Just plain Hermes will do," he said. "I'm not one of those gods who likes all that boring bowing and scraping. Now, I hear old Hades has snaffled you for some important medical work. Hephaestus thought you might want a bit of company on the first bit of the road. Tricky place to get through, the Underworld. Especially since Heracles . . ." He scowled. "Well, anyway, we're all relying on you to fix things down there."

"Me? Fix things?" said Demon. He had a nasty sinking feeling as he asked the next question. "Uh, what exactly am I supposed to fix? Hades just said he had a sick hound. What's that horrible Heracles got to do with it?" Demon had a serious grudge against Heracles, who was always trying to kill the immortal beasts.

Hermes laughed again. "Sick hound? Oh, that's a good one. I never knew my uncle Hades had a sense of humor. The beast is certainly sick, but he's not exactly a hound. Anyway, you need to get there as quick as you can. I'm sure Hades will fill you in on what Heracles did when we arrive. Iris, take us down to that side gate no one uses anymore. It's the fastest way in."

With stomach-churning suddenness, the wisp of colored nothingness dropped downward, and Demon was suddenly concentrating too hard on not being sick to ask any more questions. Just when he thought he was going to lose the battle, there was a thump, the rainbow ropes loosened, and he fell forward. A strong arm caught him just before he hit the ground and set him on his feet.

"Here we are," said Hermes. "Welcome to the side gate of the Underworld—or Hell, as some of the northerners like to call it." They were outside the entrance to a very large cave. Long coils of green-gray moss and old spiderwebs hung from its top and all around the sagging iron gates on both sides, making it look like an old man's toothless mouth surrounded by straggly silver whiskers. Although the sun shone outside, dark fingers of mist reached out from the cave mouth and clung to Demon's and Hermes's feet. The fingers had covered the silver box almost entirely, when Demon felt them wrap around his ankles and drag him forward. Then the clammy fingers started to crawl up his legs.

"Hey!" he yelled. "Stop it!" He tried to run backward out of their grasp, but they clung even harder. He began to panic and thrashed around in his efforts to escape. Then the dank tendrils touched the hand wearing Hades's ring. Immediately the mist fingers shriveled and shrank back into the cave mouth.

"That's it," said Hermes. "Show

them their master's ring. Should get you in and out of most places down here. All we have to do now is get past the angry ghosts."

"A-a-angry ghosts?" Demon asked in a small voice. He didn't like the sound of that. "Couldn't you just take me straight to Hades, Hermes? Please?"

"Now where would be the fun in that?" Hermes said. "I'll get you past the ghosts, but then I've got to go and do a bit of business with some dead heroes. I'll give you one tip, though: Hephaestus told me to tell you that the box will help if you get into a tight spot. You just have to access the special features. Now come on. It doesn't do to keep Charon the Ferryman waiting. Follow me!"

With a playful hoot of laughter, he darted forward into the darkness. Demon followed at a run. He had no choice. Only Hermes knew the way. The sole comfort he had was the silver box waddling and hopping along behind him, special features and all. He shuddered, too scared to look back, and ran on through the twisting loops and turns of the steep passage. The god's staff gave out a faint greenish-gold light that reflected off the black stone walls. There was a familiar damp smell of dead things in the air, which got stronger and stronger the deeper into the earth they traveled. Demon could hear a roaring noise up ahead, and suddenly he and Hermes burst out onto the banks of the River Styx. Across the river was an enormous crowd of spectral gray shapes, howling and moaning. Some were flinging themselves into the water, but as Demon watched, the water formed itself into lips that sucked them in and spat them back onto dry land. Others were tearing at each other, ripping off arms and heads in a bloodless frenzy of viciousness. As each ghostly limb or head dropped to the ground, it rose into the air and reaffixed itself to its spectral body. These ghosts were clearly very angry indeed.

"D-do we h-have to g-get through THEM?" Demon stuttered. His legs and arms started to shake uncontrollably, and his heart was trying to climb out of his body. Being torn apart by furious ghosts while still alive would definitely be worse than being shriveled into a little heap of ash by a god, he thought.

"Yep," said Hermes cheerfully. "But don't worry. I have a trick or two up my godly sleeves."

Then he cupped his hands around his mouth. "Yo! Charon, you old lazybones. Get that ferry over here double-time. Two passengers bound for Hades." A long black boat materialized from the opposite bank. The ferryman's staff dipped in and out of the water without so much as a ripple. As the boat slid up beside them, Hermes leaped lightly over the bow and held out a hand to Demon. "On you get, young Pandemonius."

The boat rocked slightly as Demon stepped aboard, and then there was a thump as the silver box stumbled on behind him and fell heavily onto its side. "System reboot, system reboot," it said in a faint metallic shriek, blue sparks escaping from the slightly open lid.

The small legs retracted, and with a click and a hiss, the box fell silent. Demon had no time to worry about it, though, as Charon stood up and loomed over him, holding out a hand, palm upward. It was a long, bony hand, almost fleshless, with yellow nails like horny talons.

"Pay the ferryman," he croaked. Demon fumbled desperately in the hanging pocket inside his tunic and came out with two copper obols, trying not to touch the withered skin as he handed them over. Without another word Charon tossed the coins overboard into the river. As they sank beneath the surface of the still water, he pushed off with his staff. The shrieking ghosts drew nearer and nearer, and now Demon could see that they all had bloodred eyes and sharp, pointed teeth. Demon began to shake again. They were the scariest things he'd ever seen, and he didn't want to be anywhere near them. He gave the river a desperate look. Maybe if he jumped in and swam downriver . . .

"Don't even think about it, Pandemonius," said Hermes, giving him a sharp look and grabbing his arm. "The waters of the Styx do strange things to half-mortals. You wouldn't want to end up serving Hades forever as a ghostly beetle boy, now would you?"

Charon cackled. It wasn't a friendly sound.

"N-no," said Demon. "But I also don't want to go anywhere near those horrible ghosts. Why are they so angry, anyway?"

"They're the souls of the murdered dead, seeking a way back into life to get revenge on their unpunished killers in the upper world," said Hermes, letting go of him. "Can't blame them, really, poor things, but I agree they're not very nice. Now, grab hold of the end of my staff in one hand and that box in the other, and be ready to move as soon as we hit the bank. We'll need to be quick."

Demon bent down to grab the handle of the box, which lay still and dead in the bottom of the boat. "Any special features would be welcome right about NOW," he said hopefully.

The box woke up immediately, beeped once, and began to flash silver and blue. "Initiating solo pteronautics mode," it said in its annoying tinny voice. Just as Demon tugged on the handle to try to lift it, it shot up off the floor of the boat, suddenly light as a feather, pulling his arm up with it, so Demon dangled from one hand, legs kicking in the empty air beneath him. Large, bright blue wings erupted from the box's sides, flapping frantically as the box listed to one side under Demon's weight. The handle he was holding glowed bright red, and he let go with a yell and dropped heavily to the deck, sucking his burned fingers.

"Error code 781. Passenger mode disabled," it beeped at him as he lay there, slightly stunned.

"Quick," shouted Hermes again, his voice sounding frantic. "Grab my staff." They hit the bank with a jolt, and the angry ghosts began to swarm aboard. Charon beat them off with his staff, laying about him left and right as he knocked them over the sides. Without even thinking, Demon launched himself at Hermes's staff and seized it in both hands. The golden snakes wrapped themselves around his wrists. Suddenly he and Hermes were zooming upward, following the blue trails of sparks coming out of the now-flying box. Demon felt an icy cold hand wrench at his bare ankle, and then it was gone and they were soaring over the heads of the angry ghosts. Wails of rage followed them for what seemed like miles. Then, quite suddenly, they vanished. Demon, Hermes, and the box soared downward toward a barren landscape of pure silver-gray. The god's sandals were just above Demon's head. He saw that, like the box, they had wings, white ones with golden tips. As Hermes landed, Demon noticed an earthshaking noise far off to his left. It sounded like something was sneezing its head off. A ginormous something. At each sneeze, the ground trembled under his feet, and afterward a dreadful howling filled the air.

"What's THAT?" Demon asked.

"THAT is your new patient," said Hermes.

"It definitely doesn't sound like a hound," Demon said apprehensively. Anything that shook the earth when it sneezed was not going to be like any dog he'd ever come across, that was for sure.

"Told you it wasn't," said Hermes. Then he sniffed the air. "I'd better be going now. I smell the lovely graveyard whiff of my uncle, and he doesn't really approve of me. Not much for fun and jokes, old Hades. The palace is that way." Putting a hand on Demon's shoulder, he pointed to a small uphill path between the rocks. "So long, kid. We're all counting on you. Oh, and remember, whatever happens, DON'T EAT ANYTHING DOWN HERE." Then he put on his silver helmet and disappeared. Demon was all alone in the Underworld, and the silver box had just flapped over the horizon.

CHAPTER 5

THE GUARDIAN OF THE UNDERWORLD

Demon set off at a run, scrambling up and over the pale rocks. Now he, too, could smell the unmistakable reek of death wafting toward him on the still air. As he reached the top of the hill, he saw an extraordinary sight. Immediately below him stood a vast palace, built of smooth black granite flecked with silver, each tower, turret, and spire crowned with a rotating silver skull with ruby eyes. On each side of the palace stretched walls so high that he couldn't see over them. And there, lying chained in front of a massive pair of closed silver gates, was a beast unlike any he'd ever seen. Each of its three gigantic dog heads was crowned with a hissing mane of colorful snakes. It had a dog's body, a serpent's tail, and sharp golden-clawed lion's paws. Hovering near it was the winged box, and beside it stood Hades, glowering like a furious black cloud.

"A-AA-A-A-AA-A-CCCCHHHHHOOOOOOO! AAARRRROOOOOOOO!" Each of the beast's heads sneezed and howled over and over again in a thunderous chorus. They thumped and thudded on the ground, so that cracks were appearing all around where it lay. It was clearly exhausted.

"You're late, ssstable boy," Hades growled. "Come here NOW." Stumbling and sliding over the trembling ground, Demon forced his wobbly legs to take him toward the angry god. If the poor beast hadn't been there, he might have turned and fled. However, the sight of it lying on its side, sneezing its three heads off, and the sudden worry about what Heracles might have done to it made him braver.

"I-I'm sorry, Your High Hellishness. I got here as soon as I could." He dared to look up at Hades. "What is this beast, Your M-m-m-majestic M-mightiness? And what's the matter with it?" *At least it's still visibly alive and has all its heads attached*, he thought.

Hades looked a tiny bit less angry as he heard the obvious concern in Demon's voice. But not much. Steam was drifting out of his ears, and his eyes were glowing red.

"Thisss," he said, "is Cccerberusss, my Guardian Hound of the Underworld. That oaf Heraclesss

beat him up in a fight. Then he put a diamond chain around his neck and dragged him up to earth. He'sss never been the sssame sssinccce. It'sss all my wretched sssisssster Hera'sss fault for giving Heraclesss sssuch a ssstupid tasssk. Now my poor hound is USSSELESSS." He spat, and where the spittle landed, it hissed and smoked. Demon cringed. He really, really didn't want to be in the middle of a fight between a scary god and an even more terrifying goddess. But then Hades beckoned him closer, and as Demon edged toward him nervously, Hades snapped open a small window in the silver gates. "Look through here, ssstable boy, and sssee what happensss when the Underworld has no Guardian." Demon peered through and gasped. Far away, on a plain covered in white flowers stretching as far as the eye could see, were thousands and thousands of figures. They were not just ghosts (though there were masses of those) but a few real live humans, too. The humans were wandering around, pointing and chattering, behind a man with a red placard on a stick.

"That idiot Heraclesss left the upper gate open. Now we have LIVING HUMANSSS HERE!" His voice rose to a roar, which made the ground tremble. "There'sss a man called Georgiosss running TOURSSS! 'Meet Your Favorite Hero' is how he'sss ssselling it up there on earth. And Brother Zeusss has forbidden me to do ANYTHING about it till YOU make Cccerberusss better!

"He won't ssstop sssneezing and howling. And he'sss doing it ssso loudly and ssso often that the foundationsss of my kingdom are SSSTARTING TO CRACK!" He gestured toward the largest rift. "Sssee, ssstable boy?" he hissed.

Demon looked, trying to keep his balance as Cerberus sneezed and howled again and the ground swayed like a ship's deck underneath his feet. The rock at the bottom of the cleft was moving, too, almost as if it was a barrier someone was trying to get through.

"I-it doesn't look good, Your Hellish Hugenosity," Demon said timidly.

"DOESN'T LOOK GOOD!" Hades roared. "That'sss Tartarusss down there! TARTARUSSS!"

Demon nearly let out a terrified squeak. He already knew that Tartarus was where the horrible hundred-armed monsters were imprisoned. The ones who'd tried to defeat the gods. The ones who ate all the poo from the Stables.

Hades bent his head closer. "You sssee the problem, ssstable boy," he said in a scary whisper. "If thossse hundred-armed monsssstersss essscape, they'll dessstroy the whole world. Sssooo . . ." There was an ominous pause. Demon closed his eyes and braced himself. He pretty much knew what came next when a god was this angry.

Hades seized Demon by the shoulders. "You've got until the end of the day to find out what'sss wrong with my Guardian, ssstable boy, and cure him," he hissed. "Or I assure you, I'll put you in a worssse pit of flamesss than Ixion and roassst your toesss to cccinders. That'sss jussst for ssstartersss. After that I'll let my army of ssskeleton ghossst dragonsss chassse you and eat you over and over again for the ressst of your wretched mortal daysss . . . which I can make as long as I pleassse! How would you like THAT?"

Before Demon could answer that he wouldn't like it at all, Hades threw him to the ground with a thump and strode off into the palace. He slammed its black stone doors behind him with the sound of a funeral bell. Demon lay there, wheezing, trying to get his breath back. Offy and Yukus slithered off his neck and curled around his bruises, soothing them so that he was able to get to his feet again.

Wretched gods, he thought, not daring to say it out loud in case Hades heard him. Why did they always have to be so violent? He'd have tried his hardest to cure poor Cerberus anyway. Did Hades really think that threatening him with such awful punishments was going to help? He sighed, trying not to think of how roasted toes and being eaten by skeletal dragons would feel, and went over to his patient. Cerberus's three noses were red and running with yellow slime, and his eyes were swollen shut. The snakes that made up his manes sneezed continuously in a faint hissing chorus, punctuated by enormous volcanic *ah-choos* from the three heads. Demon stroked his rough fur.

"Poor old fellow," he said. "We'll get you well again." Cerberus just groaned weakly in between sneezes and howls. Then Demon turned to the box. "I need you," he said, "and none of your stupid word games. This is an emergency." The box flapped over and settled down beside him. Demon opened its lid, and the familiar blue symbols glowed up at him. "Tell me what's wrong with this beast dog," Demon commanded it. At once three cotton swabs on strings flew out. Working quickly, they rubbed around the six nostrils and took samples of the yellow slime, then retracted, disappearing in a flash of silver light.

"Running diagnostics . . . running diagnostics . . . running diagnostics . . . ," said the familiar metallic voice. Then there was a pause and a loud whirring sound.

"Tricephalic helionosos," said the box in its usual smug way. Demon felt like kicking it.

"Stupid thing," he said, too angry to be polite. "I TOLD you not to do that. Say it so I can understand."

"Sun," said the box, quickly flapping out of his way.

"What do you mean, 'sun'?" asked Demon. "Sun isn't an illness, is it?"

"Do I really have to spell it out?" sighed the box. "Patient is allergic to Helios's rays in all three heads. Must have had too much exposure when he was up top with Heracles. It's given him a permanent case of sneezes and earache, as well as swelling his eyes shut. He can't see, he can't hear, and he definitely can't do any guarding."

"Well, we need to cure him," said Demon. "By the end of the day. Or I'll be eaten by skeleton ghost dragons forever and ever."

The box buzzed and hummed. Then it buzzed and hummed some more. The blue symbols flickered.

"Come ON," said Demon. He looked over at the door of Hades's palace. He had the uneasy feeling that something horrible was going to come out of it at any minute. "Hurry UP!"

The blue symbols turned a vile sickly green, and a small crystal bottle rose out of the box's depths.

"Temporary stasis cure. Apply one drop on each eyelid and in each nostril," it said tinnily.

Demon seized the bottle, hurried over, and started to do as the box had told him. The drops smelled like honey. As soon as he had finished, Cerberus heaved three huge sighs, rolled over, and stopped breathing. Demon nearly stopped breathing, too.

"WHAT HAVE YOU DONE, YOU STUPID THING?" Demon yelled. The box flapped hurriedly out of the way as he frantically felt the unmoving beast's chest for a heartbeat.

"Bought you time," the box squawked sulkily. "That's what a stasis potion does. It'll keep the patient in limbo and stop him from sneezing for a while. That'll just about give you time to get the ingredients I need to make the real cure before Hades comes after you."

"Ingredients? What ingredients?" asked Demon. The box clicked, then spat out a piece of parchment with brightly colored pictures on it at Demon's feet. He bent and picked it up.

"Great," he muttered. "Three mysterious yellow petals, a fingerful of spiderweb, seven grass-of-Parnassus flowers, the toenail of a hero, a maiden's sigh, the high and low notes from a lyre—and a Cauldron of Healing." As he looked at the impossible-sounding list, Demon's heart sank lower and lower.

He dropped down to the ground despairingly beside Cerberus's still body, put his head in his hands, and groaned. He might as well call Hades to toast his toes now and be done with it. But just then, a cautious whisper came through the small window in the silver gates.

"Pandemonius! Pandemonius. Are you there?"

Demon raised his head. Only the gods called him Pandemonius—and his mother, when she was mad. Maybe Hermes had come back to help him. He got up slowly and went over to the gate, not daring to hope. When he peered through the window, he saw nothing except some wisps of white mist. Maybe Hermes was still wearing his invisibility helmet.

"Who's there?" he whispered back. "Hermes, is that you?"

"No, silly, it's me, Orpheus."

Demon frowned. There'd been an Orpheus his mother had told him about—some musician boy who'd defied Hades for the sake of love. Demon still couldn't see anybody, though, as he peered through the small gap.

"Where are you?" he asked. Gradually the wisps of mist formed into a shape right in front of his eyes—the shape of a teenage boy, carrying a musical instrument under his arm. A musical instrument? Could it be? Demon stared hard. It had a curving frame like two cow horns, with strings in between them. "Is that really a lyre?" he asked eagerly.

"Yes," said Orpheus, still a bit see-through, but now fully visible. "It is. Now come on through the gate. Quick, Pandemonius! I don't want Hades to catch me here!"

"Er, it's Demon, really," said Demon. "'Pandemonius' makes me feel like I'm in trouble."

"Well, you WILL be if you don't get through that gate RIGHT NOW!" Orpheus whispered urgently.

CHAPTER 6

THE BOY WITH THE LYRE

Demon was worried about leaving Cerberus by himself, but the box assured him that the Guardian of the Underworld would come to no harm.

"What if Hades comes out and sees him like this?" Demon asked, hesitating.

"Then you're better off not here, aren't you?" said the box in its metallic voice. "Now HURRY UP. Like Orpheus said, the clock is ticking, and you only have the rest of the day to find my ingredients."

A few moments later, Demon walked through the silver gates, closing them gently behind him with a last look back at his enormous beast dog patient, who hadn't so much as twitched a claw since having the potion. The box came flying up behind Demon, and together they met the ghostly figure pacing impatiently amid the white flowers. The red-eyed silver skulls on top of the palace swiveled to watch the two of them walk out onto the plain and then turned away.

Now Demon was truly in the land of the dead. He checked his body to see if it was still solid and human. Luckily it was. Then he took a deep breath and got a good look around for the first time. The dim twilight covered the landscape, making everything soft and blurred, as if it were not quite real. The sky (if it was a sky) had no clouds, stars, nor moon, but glowed eerie green as far as the eye could see. There were no birds overhead, only ghostly bats. The white flowers covered the ground like a carpet.

"How did you know I was here?" he burst out. He was really longing to know whether Orpheus could still play the lyre in his present form, but hesitated to ask. He'd never had a conversation with a ghost before, and he didn't want to say the wrong thing.

"Hermes said you were down here and might need a bit of assistance. Though I'm not sure how I can help, really."

Demon sent a barrowload of thankful thoughts in Hermes's direction. "Well, I can think of one thing right away," he said. Never mind politeness. "Does your lyre still work?"

"Of course it does," said Orpheus, sounding slightly offended, as Demon had feared he would. "I may be dead, but I'm still the world's

greatest musician, you know." He pulled out the instrument and strummed his fingers over the strings. The loveliest trill of music rose up into the air as Demon hurried to explain about his impossible list and about the two lyre notes he needed to help cure Cerberus.

"But how will you catch them?" asked Orpheus.

"Oh," he said. It simply hadn't occurred to him that he might need to actually catch the notes. He looked down at the box. "Any clever ideas, oh mighty chest of wisdom?" he asked it.

The box didn't answer. It just stomped over to Orpheus and shot out a long tube with a trumpet-like attachment, which fastened itself to the misty lyre like an octopus's sucker.

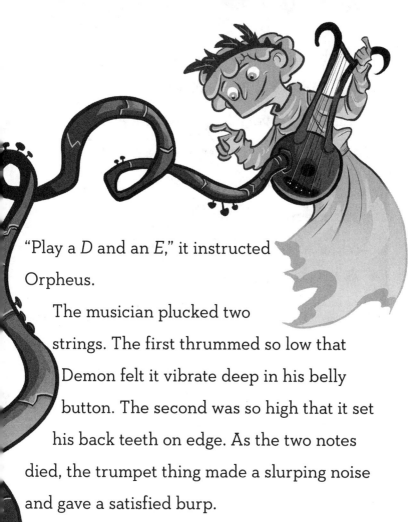

"Play a *D* and an *E*," it instructed
Orpheus.

The musician plucked two
strings. The first thrummed so low that
Demon felt it vibrate deep in his belly
button. The second was so high that it set
his back teeth on edge. As the two notes
died, the trumpet thing made a slurping noise
and gave a satisfied burp.

"Musical items retrieved and saved to disk,"
said the box as the trumpet detached itself
and slipped back inside the lid. *One ingredient
down, five more and a magic cauldron to go,*

Demon thought. Suddenly his stomach began to rumble loudly, and he realized he was hungry. It seemed like a very long time since he'd had those sausages on buns in Hestia's kitchens.

"Oh dear," said Orpheus. "I'd forgotten humans need food. That's too bad."

"What do you mean?" Demon asked.

"Well," said Orpheus, "you mustn't eat anything down here. That's how Hades caught his wife, Queen Persephone. She only ate seven pomegranate seeds, and now she has to stay down here for four months of every year. You can't let even one thing pass your lips until you return to the upper world, or you'll be Hades's prisoner forever."

Demon suddenly remembered that Hermes had told him the same thing. He decided to ignore his stomach, however much it complained. He definitely didn't want to be

Hades's prisoner for one single minute, let alone forever.

"Now show me that list," said Orpheus, holding out his insubstantial hand. Demon took it out of the folds of his tunic and handed it over at once. Unfortunately, the piece of parchment slipped right through Orpheus's fingers and drifted to the ground. Demon picked it up and held it out so that Orpheus could see the pictures.

"Hmm. Spiderwebs are easy. Arachne has lots. And grass-of-Parnassus grows by the banks of the River Lethe, just where it joins the marsh. I'm not sure about this yellow flower, but Eurydice is sure to know."

"Who's Eurydice?" Demon interrupted. Orpheus's see-through cheeks took on a slightly pink shade, as if Eos had just touched him with her fingers.

"Er, she's my girlfriend," he muttered. "Hades

is always forbidding us to be together, but we don't take much notice . . . that's why I don't want him to catch me." He cast a very nervous glance back at the silver skulls on top of the palace. "Anyway," he said, changing the subject quickly, "let's start with the hero's toenail. That shouldn't be too hard. There are at least a thousand of them down here, and it doesn't say it has to be a live hero, does it?"

"No," said Demon, "it doesn't. But where—?" He broke off, suddenly noticing that the crowds of people and ghosts he'd seen when Hades had made him look through the window of the gate were drifting toward them over the plain. There was a lot of noise going on, and the sound of a man shouting. "Might there be a hero in that bunch?" he asked.

"Almost certainly," said Orpheus. "Follow me. And try not to get trampled in the crush."

He shot forward, the bottom half of his body dissolving into mist as he did so. Demon sprinted in his wake, with the box galloping clumsily behind.

Demon felt a bit nervous. He hadn't met a hero before. Were they as scary as gods and goddesses? *Surely not*, he thought. Heroes were supposed to be good, weren't they? Then he remembered Heracles. Heracles called himself a hero, so maybe that wasn't true, after all.

Just then, Demon reached the crowd and crashed hard into the tall man called Georgios whom Hades had pointed out earlier. Up close he had a very large stomach and enormous, extremely dirty feet. All thought of heroes was knocked out of Demon's head as he tripped and landed with a bump, right on top of the box.

"Oof! Operating system overload! Operating system overload!" it squawked, spitting blue sparks. Demon got up hurriedly. He couldn't afford for it to break. There was no Heffy down here to fix it.

"What's this, what's this?" said a loud voice above him as he struggled to his feet. "I don't remember you being on my tour. Have you sneaked in without paying? Can't have that, can I?" said Georgios, waving his red placard.

"No," said Demon, indignant at the accusation. "I haven't. I'm on a job for Hades, if you must know."

The man laughed. "A likely story," he said. "A little shrimp like you on a job for His Majesty, the god of death? I don't think so, sonny. And what's that you've got there? Stolen it, have you?" He reached down for the box, but as his fingers touched it, it let out an orange flash of lightning, which made the man snatch his hand away with a shriek.

"Oops! Error code 93. That wasn't supposed to happen," said the box. It didn't sound very sorry, though. Demon felt like patting it, for once.

"Perhaps that'll teach you to believe people when they're telling the truth," he said. Georgios backed away, sucking his burned hand. He gave Demon a nasty look, waved his red placard over his head, and walked off muttering. Then he began to shout again.

"Move along, people! Move along! Follow Georgios's Underworld Tours sign! Best and only one in the business! Next stop, Achilles and Ajax." A chattering crowd fell in behind the man as Demon began to look for Orpheus. There was such a press of ghosts and people around him that he couldn't see the musician boy at all. He began to panic, but then caught sight of a misty lyre, held up high over everyone's heads, waving wildly. He began to run toward it, pushing his way between ghostly figures. They melted and flowed around (and sometimes through) him as he went, leaving him cold and shivering. He wished he'd remembered his cloak. Finally he got through to Orpheus.

"We'll never find anyone in this crowd," shouted the ghost. "Georgios's tours are making the Underworld a nightmare. Come this way!"

After more pushing and shoving, they came to a dead tree where several warrior ghosts wearing armor and carrying swords were gathered. With them was a gigantic man with a bow on his back, a belt made of faintly shining stars, and a mass of ghostly hounds at his feet.

"There's your hero," said Orpheus.

"Is that *Orion*?" whispered Demon. Orpheus nodded, so Demon marched up to him bravely. Orion had been killed by the giant scorpion,

Demon's least favorite beast in the Stables. Although Orion was a hunter, and he didn't normally like hunters, Demon had some sympathy for him. Demon had been stung by the giant scorpion, too. It hurt a lot.

"Excuse me, Your Extreme Heroicness," he said. "But could I have one of your toenails, please?"

All the warrior ghosts laughed. "You human souvenir hunters!" one of them said. "Bits from ghosts never last up in the mortal world, you know!"

"I'm not a souvenir hunter," said Demon angrily. "I'm the Official Beast Keeper to the gods. It's for a potion to cure Cerberus."

"Ah," said Orion. "Poor old Cerberus. We heard what happened. It's been chaos down here ever since. Well, if *that's* what it's for, you can certainly have one, Beast Keeper."

Orion shooed the ghost dogs away, bent down to his left foot, and pulled one of his large square toenails right off, making ghostly blood ooze onto his sandal. Immediately, a pair of pincers came out of the box and grabbed it.

"Toenail item recovered," it trilled happily.

"Thanks, Orion," Demon said gratefully, trying not to look at the misty blood pooling under the hero's foot. Then he had a thought. "Um, do you know where we could find a maiden's sigh, by any chance?" he asked. Orion and the others snickered.

"Orpheus here will help you with that," Orion said, winking. "He's got a few maidens sighing after him."

Orpheus blushed again. "Shhh!" he said. "Stop teasing me. You know there's only one I care about. Come on, Demon, let's go and find Eurydice."

Just four things to go now, Demon thought as they walked away from the laughing warriors. Maybe he could do this in one day, after all.

It took ages to reach the grove where Eurydice lived, but they got there at last. She was a tall, beautiful ghost with long hair down to her knees. Getting her to sigh into the box's trumpet attachment was easy. She just had to look at Orpheus. Demon stared at the two of them in disgust while they hugged and kissed as if they hadn't seen each other for years.

He didn't get this being-in-love thing at all.

"Ahem," he said at last, clearing his throat loudly. "Spiderwebs? Yellow petals? Grass-of-Parnassus? Cauldron of Healing?" The two lovers took absolutely no notice of him, gazing into each other's eyes goopily.

"I STILL NEED FOUR THINGS TO CURE CERBERUS!" he yelled at last. Both Orpheus and Eurydice jumped a foot into the air and then dissolved into streamers of mist.

"Don't DO that!" said Orpheus's voice indistinctly. "I thought Hades had caught us for a minute. Now we'll have to disentangle ourselves."

Tapping his foot impatiently, Demon waited while the two lovers sorted themselves out. "Now," he said. "Are you going to help me find the other things or not?"

CHAPTER 7

THE SPINNER'S CAVE

"Ooh!" said Eurydice, clapping her ghostly hands as she looked at Demon's list. They made no sound. "That's Cerberus's new flower!"

"Cerberus's new flower? What do you mean?"

"The wolfsbane petals. It was when Heracles was dragging him back down here from earth," said Eurydice. "I was coming out of Arachne's cave, and I saw it. Wherever his drool touched the ground, little yellow flowers sprang up, just like buttercups. They were so pretty. I've never seen a color like that down here before. It's all horrid old gray and black and that icky green sky."

"Could you take me there?" Demon asked eagerly.

Eurydice made a face. "It's a long way. And Arachne was quite mean to me last time I visited."

"We need to get spiderwebs from Arachne, anyway," said Orpheus. "She's only mean because she has all those arms and legs now. And we can take the shortcut past Lethe's marsh. Come on, it's important. Like a hero's quest or something."

"Please," begged Demon. He was very aware of the clock ticking away. He wriggled his toes uncomfortably.

"Oh, all right," said Eurydice. "I don't mind

Arachne really. But don't blame me if Lethe gets you. She's scary. We'll have to try to go past very quietly without her noticing."

Sometime later, Demon was trying to ignore his grumbling stomach as they trudged along in silent single file along a squelchy gray path beside a marsh. He was so hungry he would have eaten dirt if someone had given him a plate of it. *Don't eat, don't eat* was the monotonous refrain that accompanied his heavy footsteps. There was almost no one around in this part of the Underworld, apart from the ever-present ghost bats. Demon liked bats. There'd been a colony near his home in Arcadia. As he craned his head upward, trying to listen to what they were saying, he tripped over his own feet and fell into the marshy water on his hands and knees. There was a sudden stink of old, unwashed socks.

"Ugh," he spluttered. Just as he began to scramble out, a bony hand grabbed his wrist, nails digging into his flesh like claws.

"Not so fast," said a harsh voice, bubbling up from the water. Eurydice moaned with terror and hid behind Orpheus, who was holding his lyre like a weapon. Demon shook his wrist over and over again, trying to get free, but it was no good. The hand had him in an iron grip. Then the marsh plopped and bubbled as a terrible figure rose out of it, draped with slimy gray waterweed robes.

"What do we have here?" she snarled through a mouth full of sharp pointed teeth. "A half-mortal boy, two ghosts, and"—she peered over Demon's shoulder—"a silver box with legs?"

Demon's heart was pounding like one of Hephaestus's hammers. This must be Lethe, spirit of forgetfulness. "I-I-I'm sorry, Your

Magnificent Marshiness," he stuttered.

Lethe smiled at him. It was not a nice smile. "Ohhhh! You WILL be," she said. "You'll be sorrier than a squashed scorpion." She began to pull him down into the marsh. Demon felt himself begin to sink.

"Noooo!" he wailed. "Orpheus, help me!"

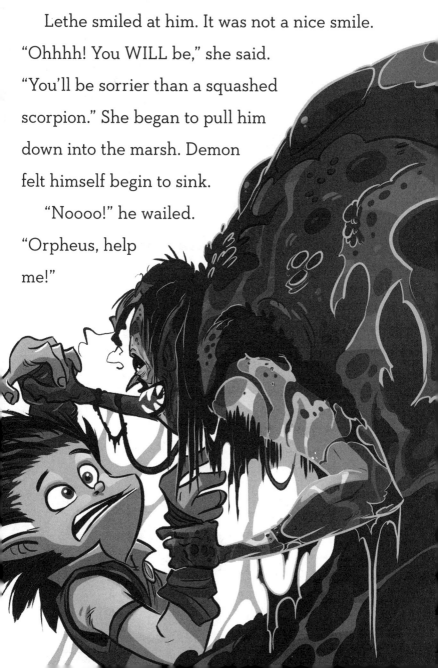

Right then Orpheus began to play his lyre. Then he began to sing. It was the saddest song Demon had ever heard. As the sorrowful notes wove around them, Lethe's grip slackened, and Demon scrabbled backward toward the path. Fiery blue tears started to run down her cheeks and set the oily surface of the water aflame.

"Ahh!" she sighed. "Now you've spoiled all my fun, Orpheus. You know I can't resist your music." Orpheus kept on playing as Demon hauled himself out and tried to scrape off the gray ooze as best he could. When Orpheus's song came to an end, Lethe took a gliding step toward them through the burning water. Demon cowered. Eurydice was right. She was very scary, indeed.

"Oh, do stop cringing, boy," she said irritably. "Tell me why you were creeping past my marsh like a thief in the night."

Demon explained about Cerberus, his voice still trembling.

"Very well," said Lethe. "For Cerberus's sake I will let you pass this time. But if you ever come this way again, I shall demand a price. I will take your most precious memory from you. It will not be a pleasant experience."

Demon nodded. He would have agreed to anything to get out of there. He'd just noticed that the sky had grown a little darker. How long did he have before his day ran out? Then he noticed that Lethe was holding a bunch of delicate five-petaled white flowers out to him. "You may need these," she said.

Behind him, the box opened its lid. "Insert floral items here, please," it said, more polite than Demon had ever heard it. It was the grass-of-Parnassus that Demon needed for the potion, and now there were only three things left to find!

As they left Lethe behind, Eurydice was full of how brave and clever Orpheus had been. She went on and on about it as Demon stumbled up the high rocky hills that led to Arachne's cave. He wished she'd shut up, but he knew he needed her to show him Cerberus's flowers, so he didn't say so. Finally, as they came over one more summit, he saw a bright patch of yellow on the hillside below.

"That's them!" Eurydice cried when they were about halfway down.

Demon raced down the hill, almost slipping in his eagerness, picked three yellow petals, and brought them back to the box, which was ready and waiting beside Orpheus and Eurydice.

"Insert fl—"

"I know," said Demon. "Insert floral items here. I'm not stupid, you know."

"Could have fooled me," muttered the box

crossly, trailing along as they climbed higher and higher up the mountainside. Suddenly, Demon began to feel a stickiness under his feet. *Schlurp schlap schlurp* went his sandals. He looked down. Trails of thick slime covered the path.

"What's this?" he asked.

"Hush," said Eurydice. "You'll soon see. But don't mention it in front of Arachne. She doesn't like to talk about it." The stickiness got worse as they reached the entrance to Arachne's cave, and now Demon could hear a regular clicking and clunking coming from inside.

Orpheus rang a little bell by the entrance.

"Who's there?" said a silvery voice.

"Orpheus and Eurydice," said Orpheus. "And we've brought someone to see you."

"Come in then," said Arachne. "And mind the tapestries."

As Demon stepped into the cave and saw what was inside, his eyes nearly bugged right out of his head. There crouched an enormous gray spider, her eight legs busy weaving on four different looms, shuttles flying faster than his eyes could follow. There was a mass of different-colored thread spooling out from her spinnerets, along with a lot of sticky stuff that covered the whole floor with a thick, gluey coating. What was even odder was that the spider had the face of a pretty girl.

From each loom hung beautiful tapestries of all the gods and goddesses. There was Zeus with his thunderbolts, there was Hera, and there was Heffy at his forge.

The pictures were all slightly irreverent, though. Zeus was wearing a silly hat, Hera was sitting backward on a donkey, and Heffy was using a chicken instead of a hammer.

"Wow!" Demon said. "They're amazing! You must be very brave to weave *those*!"

It was just the right thing to say. Arachne beamed. "Ooh!" she squealed. "How nice of you to say so." Then she frowned. "But how does a mortal boy come to be down here?"

Demon explained about Cerberus yet again. "All we need now are some spiderwebs," he said. "And a Cauldron of Healing."

"Help yourself to webs," said Arachne, gesturing with one spindly leg to the corner. "I have plenty to spare." So Demon gathered up handfuls of the multicolored thread, getting himself hopelessly stuck together as he did so. The box clearly didn't like having sticky feet, so it had taken to the air again, wings flapping. Orpheus and Eurydice huddled away from the gusts of air, trying to hold their bodies together, as two long mechanical arms appeared under the box's wings and unraveled Demon, turning him around and around as it made the web strands into a neat rope.

"Web item retrieved and stored to memory," its tinny voice said.

"Did you say you needed a Cauldron of Healing?" Arachne asked when he was slightly less stuck together.

Demon nodded. "Do you know where I could find one down here?"

"We-e-e-lll . . . ," said Arachne slowly. "I'd normally send you up to Chiron the centaur in the mortal world. But down here . . ." She shook her head, and Demon's heart sank into his sandals again.

"Do you think Queen Persephone might have one?" Orpheus asked. "She's a healer, isn't she?"

Suddenly Eurydice started jumping up and down. "You're so clever, Orphy! I think I've seen one in her chambers," she squealed. "That time Hades made me be her lady-in-waiting, remember? She made a potion in it to mend one of the Skeleton Guard's arms."

"D-does that mean I have to go into Hades's palace?" asked Demon, dreading the answer and wondering nervously what a Skeleton Guard was.

"I'm afraid it does," said Orpheus. "And I don't think you've got much time left. Look!" He gestured at the cave entrance.

Demon looked outside. It was much darker.

"Two hours three minutes and twenty seconds, two hours three minutes and nineteen seconds, two hours three minutes and eighteen seconds," the box chimed in helpfully.

Demon glared at it.

"Let's get going, then," he said through gritted teeth.

CHAPTER 8

THE PALACE OF DEATH

It was one of the most uncomfortable journeys of Demon's entire life. The box had grudgingly agreed to enable its special passenger mode for him. It even provided a large bottle for Orpheus to pour himself into so he didn't blow away during the ride. After many tearful farewells from Eurydice, who was staying to visit with Arachne for a while, Demon lay across the box's silver lid. He clung on to Orpheus's bottle with one hand and the handle with the other. The large blue wings flapped frantically, once, twice, three times, and then they were airborne.

"Good-bye, Orphy!" sobbed Eurydice.

"Good luck, Demon!" called Arachne.

Demon slipped and slid from side to side, terrified that he was going to fall off as the box labored across Lethe's marsh and veered sharply right.

Then it plunged downward, avoiding a cloud of ghostly bats.

"*Ow! Ow! Ow!*" Demon howled as his toes scraped along the ground. The box merely let out a stream of blue symbols that roared past his ears, crackling and spitting with sparks. It rose unsteadily into the air again with an unbalancing wobble that nearly caused Demon to drop Orpheus's bottle. Over Eurydice's grove, over the warriors' tree, over the crowded plain of ghosts they flew, until Demon could finally see the black walls of Hades's palace. With one last mighty effort, the box heaved itself and Demon over the silver gates and flumped down beside Cerberus's body with a crash. As Demon thudded to the ground, the silver skulls on top of the palace roofs swiveled to look at him. Their fiery eyes suddenly ignited, pinning Demon in the middle of a circle of hot red beams.

"Intruder alert! Intruder alert! Intruder alert!" shrieked the skulls, their bony jaws creaking like rusty hinges.

"Quick!" said Orpheus's muffled voice from inside the bottle. "Show them your ring!" Demon got his hand out from underneath him and waved Hades's black ring at them. As soon as it touched one of the red beams, they all winked out.

"False alarm! Stand down, boys!" said the nearest skull. Demon looked around nervously. Had Hades heard them? He hoped not. He jumped to his feet, wincing at the pain from his rough landing. How much time did he have left before the god came after him? He HAD to find that cauldron quickly.

Offy and Yukus were just slithering down his legs and starting to mend him when he noticed all three of Cerberus's noses twitching.

"Oh no," he said to the box. "I think he's going to—"

"*AAHHCHHOOOOO AAHHCHHOOOOO AAHHCHHOOOOO AAAAARRROOOOO!*"

The three heads crashed to the ground,

making it shake and shudder. A deep new crack snaked out underneath them, and out of it came the sound of a thousand hungry hundred-armed monsters.

"Box!" shouted Demon. "Do something! Please!"

The silver lid flew open and the silver disk on a tube shot out, attaching itself to Cerberus's heaving chest. It then retracted into the box like a whip, and the box snapped shut.

"Sneezing symptoms should not have resumed yet. Running emergency diagnostics," it shrieked. Demon clenched his fists, trying not to panic. The snakes of Cerberus's manes were beginning to sway and stir. Then the box lid lifted again. A large glass tube with a thin pointy quill on one end and a ring on the other popped up from its depths.

"Inject patient's heart with contents of syringe," squawked the box. "Hurry!"

Demon didn't understand. "What do you MEAN?" he screamed.

"Stick him with the pointy end and push!" Its metallic voice rose to a screech. So Demon grabbed the glass tube and ran over to Cerberus. He felt desperately for his heartbeat as he saw the six nostrils twitch again ominously.

Thuddity thud thuddity thud! There it was. He jabbed the pointy end between the ribs and pushed down on the ring, which slid down into the tube with a hiss. Cerberus's body jerked once and then lay still again. Demon sat back on his heels, listening nervously to the furious bellowing coming out of the crack to his left.

"Emergency averted," said the box smugly. "You have precisely one hour to complete your task." The blue symbols inside flashed twice, and then the lid shut with a bang. "Battery recharge pending. Shutdown imminent." It sighed deeply, made a strange pinging sound, and went totally silent.

"Nooooo!" Demon yelled, shaking it by both handles and rattling the lid. "You can't go to sleep NOW!" But the box remained a lifeless silver lump. Nothing Demon said or did would wake it up. Finally, almost speechless with terror and frustration, he remembered to let Orpheus out of his bottle.

"What am I going to DO?" he asked as the mist flowed out and re-formed into his ghostly friend. The box had been his savior so often that he didn't know how he was going to manage without its tinny advice.

"Steal the cauldron, get back here quick, and hope it recovers," said Orpheus. "Didn't you hear it? We have less than an hour. Come on!" He flowed toward the black stone doors of the palace, Demon running beside him. One touch of Hades's ring on the doors and they opened. They were in!

Edging around the sides of a large courtyard with a dead weeping willow and a sluggish fountain in the center, Orpheus put a finger to his lips.

"This way, I think," he whispered, leading Demon into a wide passageway lined with unmoving giant stone skeletons that stared silently at one another across the shiny marble. Demon looked at them uneasily as he tiptoed past, but they didn't move a fingerbone. His thumping heartbeat ticked away the seconds as they ran up narrow black marble staircases and down broad, empty corridors. Then, just as Demon smelled the scent of new-mown hay—surprising in that musty place—they heard the sound of muffled marching footsteps.

"Quick! Behind here!" Orpheus hissed,

disappearing into an alcove behind a black velvet curtain. Demon slipped in with him, feeling the clammy mist of the ghostly body touch his side. He peeked out through a tiny crack to see a terrifying sight. A whole platoon of the giant stone skeletons had come to life and was marching in perfect step down the corridor, bones clicking softly as they passed.

"What are THEY?" Demon whispered, though he feared he knew. Immediately, the skeletons stopped dead, skulls turning toward the alcove as one. Demon froze, not daring to move even an eyelash, let alone breathe. Seeing nothing, they marched on, rows and rows of them. Demon let out a whooshing breath as the last of them disappeared.

"Phew!" he said.

"Definitely phew! Those were Hades's personal Skeleton Guard," Orpheus replied.

"The ones Eurydice was talking about. We passed the spares on the way. Didn't you notice?"

"I thought they were just statues," Demon said. Then he smelled the new-mown hay again. The scent seemed to be coming from a door just ahead. A door with a silver crown and a wheat stalk over it. "Hey! Are those Queen Persephone's chambers?" he asked. She was the goddess of spring and growing things, after all, as well as Hades's wife.

"Yes, they are. Wait there! I'm just going to make sure there's nobody inside," said Orpheus, flitting across the corridor. Demon jiggled from foot to foot impatiently, but soon Orpheus was beckoning him forward.

"Coast's clear," he said. "I think they're usually in the big hall at this time of day, judging the dead. Either one of the gods is on your side, or you're very lucky!"

Demon sent a quick thought of thanks to Heffy, Hestia, and Hermes, just in case. If any gods were going to be on his side, they were.

Queen Persephone's chambers were a riot of color, festooned with flowers so bright that they almost hurt Demon's eyes after all the gray and black. He suddenly realized how much he missed Olympus and the Stables. Were his beasts all right? Was Doris the Hydra cleaning out the poo properly and feeding everyone? But there was no time to think of that. The clock was ticking, and they needed to find that cauldron urgently. Demon and Orpheus moved quickly through the rooms, searching. Eurydice hadn't been able to remember exactly where she'd seen it. "There were pretty berries near it, I think," she'd said. "Red ones like lots of tiny cherries."

There wasn't a berry in sight in any of the

rooms. Not a single one. Demon was in despair, looking under drifts of poppies and behind clumps of bluebells.

"We'll never find it," he groaned. Even the normally cheerful Orpheus looked glum.

"It's all spring flowers in here," he said. "Maybe my Eurydice got it wrong."

Suddenly Demon had an inspiration.

"What if Queen Persephone had her autumn decorations up when Eurydice was here?" he asked. "This definitely looks like spring, but tiny red berries come in autumn from trees like mountain ash and hawthorn. Maybe we should be looking for those kinds of blossom." So they searched every tree in the place. There was cherry blossom and apple blossom, pear blossom and plum blossom, but they couldn't find a single hawthorn or mountain ash. Demon was about to tear his hair out with frustration,

when his eyes fell on a little tree with shiny
reddish bark and clouds of tiny white flowers,
half-hidden behind a high wall covered in ferns.
Between its moss-covered roots was a glint of
gold. Demon ran over and pulled at it with a
shout of triumph. Out came a tiny cauldron with
a silver handle.

"Got it!" he cried. Just then there was a
tremor beneath his feet, and a muffled rumble.
"Oh no! I think Cerberus has started sneezing
again! RUN!"

CHAPTER 9

THE CAULDRON OF HEALING

Demon and Orpheus ran at top speed back the

way they'd come, avoiding more

marching Skeleton Guards by the skin of their teeth, and burst out through the black stone doors again.

"Box! Box! Wake up! I've got the Cauldron of Healing!" Demon shouted, just as three enormous sneezes and howls shook the earth again.

The box woke up with a screech, glowed blue, grabbed the cauldron from Demon with its mechanical arm, and scuttled toward Cerberus. "Implementing potion interface, implementing potion interface," it gabbled, vibrating so fast that it became a silver blur.

With a burst of foul gas, several scaly green arms erupted out of the crack in the ground near Demon's feet. "AARRGGH!" Demon screamed, jumping for cover behind Cerberus's huge body as the arms grabbed at him. Orpheus slipped in beside him as a smudge of mist.

"What's happening?" Orpheus shouted. There was no time for Demon to answer. Instead he pointed with a shaking finger at the black doors, which had just crashed open. A whole platoon of Skeleton Guards came pouring out, stone swords raised, and started hacking at the scaly arms. Green blood poured over the dusty ground, smoking and bubbling, and the roars turned to shrieks of agony as more arms reached out from the cracks.

Demon was trying hard not to panic amid the chaos happening around him. He watched the box like a hawk, willing it to hurry. After a moment, the box snapped open, and then the small golden cauldron was floating up out of its inside, filled with a liquid that glowed bright purple.

"Patient must ingest potion immediately, patient must ingest potion immediately," it beeped loudly. Demon seized the cauldron by the silver handle and started pouring the purple liquid between each of Cerberus's three jaws in turn.

"Don't sneeze, don't sneeze, don't sneeze," he muttered over and over again as he worked faster than he ever had before. As Cerberus slobbered and dribbled and swallowed, the yellow oozy slime miraculously disappeared from around each of his six nostrils. He opened his suddenly unswollen eyes, got up, and shook himself, making Demon roll hurriedly out of the way of his enormous lion's paws. Three huge

heads gazed down at him. Three huge tongues lolled out between hundreds of sharp white teeth, dripping poisonous beast dog slobber, which burned holes as it hit the ground.

"Thank you, stable boy," said three booming dog voices and a thousand hissing snake ones.

"N-no problem," said Demon nervously, backing away slightly.

Then Cerberus raised his heads and sniffed the air.

"WOOF! WOOF! WOOF!" he bayed out of all three mouths, charging at the silver gate, which flew open as he hit it. Demon and Orpheus stared as Cerberus raced toward the plain, barking all the way. Suddenly there was a cacophony of human yells and screams, and they watched Georgios, the annoying tour guide, fling his red placard away as he took to his heels and ran as fast as he could, stomach wobbling before him.

"Serves him right," said Orpheus unsympathetically. "Humans aren't meant to come to the Underworld while they're still alive. I hope Cerberus eats him."

"I do ssso agree with you, dear Orpheusss," said a soft, sibilant voice behind them. "But it'sss not Georgiosss'sss time to die yet. My Guardian will sssimply play with him for a while, then herd him and his cussstomersss back to the upper world." Demon whirled around and fell to his knees as Hades dropped a black-gauntleted hand on his shoulder. Orpheus dissolved into a streak of mist and disappeared through the open gates with a ghostly moan of fear.

"Jussst in time, ssstable boy. Jussst in time. My ghossst dragonsss *will* be disssappointed. Are you sure you wouldn't like to give them sssome sssatisssfaction? After all, you did ssso nearly fail to cure my Guardian in time. Look at how the monssstersss almossst got out."

Demon shuddered. "N-n-no th-thank you, Y-y-your D-deathly I-illustriousness, I-I'll p-pass." Over Hades's shoulder, he could see a few of the Skeleton Guards still battling the last few monster arms. Their gray stone bones were spattered with green blood. The rest were busy filling in the cracks in the ground and throwing cut-off arms back down where they had come from. It was a gruesome sight.

Hades looked slyly at Demon. "Very well," he said. "But I must insssissst you come to a little feassst with me and my dear queen. I'm sure you're VERY hungry by now!" Demon gulped, willing his stomach not to rumble. He was STARVING, but he knew he couldn't accept the god of death's invitation. What could he say? Would Hades fry him to a crisp if he refused? There was an uncomfortable silence as Demon thought feverishly.

"There'll be ssstuffed vine leavesss and roasssted sssalmon and honey cakesss," Hades said temptingly. Demon's mouth watered. Could it really do any harm? Just one little honey cake? Just a tiny piece of salmon? He was about to open his mouth to say yes, when an invisible hand clamped over it and prevented him.

"Hello, dear Uncle Hades," said Hermes, pulling off his invisibility helmet and popping into view, giving Demon a stern shake. "Must rush. Zeus wants his stable boy back. Preferably in one piece. So kind of you to invite him to dinner, but he'll have to decline."

He seized Demon under one arm, whisked
the silver box under the other, and tossed his
helmet back onto his head. With a whoosh,
they rose into the air and zoomed away, leaving
Hades hissing and screaming with frustration
and rage behind them.

"Wretched
messsenger," he
howled. "Jussst
wait till I get
my handsss on
you! I WANTED
that ssstable boy!"

"Lucky I was around," said Hermes. "Or you might have been in *real* trouble."

Demon let out the breath he'd been holding ever since Hermes had picked him up. His heart felt as if it were trying to crawl out from under his ribs. He imagined being stable boy to Hades and shivered. It would have been TERRIBLE.

"Thank you, Hermes," he said gratefully.

"Hey, think nothing of it," replied the god, snickering slightly. "Anything to annoy old Death Face."

Demon swallowed. "W-will Hades come after me again?" he asked.

"No no, don't worry, Pandemonius. It's me he's angry with. But I'd avoid him for a while just the same."

Demon vowed silently to do just that.

CHAPTER 10

THE STABLES AGAIN

Demon tried to look down at himself. It was a very odd experience being invisible. He could feel his body perfectly well, and he could feel Hermes's arm around his waist. He just couldn't see anything except the landscape below. He drew his legs up at the sight of the angry ghosts milling around on the banks of the Styx.

"I think we'll give old Charon a miss this time," said Hermes. "I wasn't lying when I said Zeus wants you back quickly. The Stables are starting to smell again. Aphrodite is complaining that all her nightdresses stink of poo."

"Oh no!" Demon exclaimed. "What happened? I left Doris the Hydra in charge. It was supposed to clean up and feed everyone."

"Ah!" said Hermes. "The Hydra, eh? Well, I'm sorry to tell you it's had a little problem."

Demon clutched the invisible arm holding him as they swerved around the corners of the dark tunnels. "W-what problem?" he asked, his starving stomach beginning to feel a bit queasy.

"Apparently it, uh, snacked on a bit too much ambrosia cake itself instead of giving it to the other beasts. It's been lying in its pen moaning with a bad stomachache ever since you left."

"Oh! Poor thing!" said Demon. "It's not really very smart. Maybe it misunderstood me." He hated to think of any of his beasts being in pain or discomfort. "Can Iris take us back really quickly? I need to give it something from the box."

Quite soon, he wished he hadn't asked that question. The fast version of the Iris Express was even more scary and sickening than the normal one. His whole face felt as if it were being torn off backward as they zoomed up at warp speed. He fell out onto the warm, sunbaked earth of Olympus gasping and wheezing. Hermes gently placed the box beside him.

"I've got another message to deliver," he said. "See you around!" And with that, he was gone again. The familiar smell of beast poo drifted into Demon's nostrils as he hauled himself upright and wobbled off toward the Stables, the box in his arms.

"About time, Pan's scrawny kid," said the griffin grumpily from its post beside the Hydra's pen. "I'm STARVING!"

"FOOD FOOD FOOD FOOD!" went a chorus of barks, moos, baas, squeals, squeaks, hisses, and neighs.

"ALL RIGHT!" Demon yelled. "I'll feed you as soon as I've mended Doris!" He looked at the box. "Come on," he said. "A Hydra stomachache should be easy after what we've just been through."

Ten minutes later the Hydra was sleeping contentedly, little whuffling snores coming out of its nine heads, and Demon was busy shoveling ambrosia cake and golden hay into mangers. Soon there was the sound of happy chomping. His own stomach was grumbling urgently as he went to get his wheelbarrow, brush, and shovel. Could he risk popping over to Hestia's kitchen to see if there was a spare something he could eat? No, he decided. He didn't want Aphrodite complaining again. The fewer gods and goddesses who wanted to turn him into little piles of ash, the better. He stuffed several pieces of ambrosia cake into his mouth at once and chewed them down thankfully. They didn't taste half bad after a whole day of Underworld adventures.

Demon tipped barrowload after barrowload down the poo chute, but there was a deathly hush from the hundred-armed monsters below. Maybe they were too busy regrowing the arms the Skeleton Guard had cut off, he thought, feeling a little bit sorry for them. He swept and shoveled till he was totally exhausted, only just avoiding the giant scorpion's stinger, which made him think of Orion down in the Underworld. He wondered how Orpheus was doing, too, feeling sad that they hadn't had a chance to say good-bye. When the Stables were spick-and-span again, he put all his tools away and slumped down on a bale of golden hay, feeling Helios's rays warming him through.

"Pleased to be back?" asked the griffin, coming out of the Stables and pecking him gently on the shoulder.

"SO pleased," said Demon, with an enormous yawn, snuggling up against its warm yellow body. "Home at last," he mumbled drowsily as his eyes closed.

"I wouldn't get too comfortable, stable boy," the griffin whispered in his ear. "Another Important Visitor turned up here last night."

But Demon was fast asleep and didn't hear him.

GLOSSARY

PRONUNCIATION GUIDE

THE GODS

Aphrodite (AF-ruh-DY-tee): Goddess of love and beauty and all things pink and fluffy.

Dionysus (DY-uh-NY-suss): God of wine. Turns even sensible gods into silly goons.

Eos (EE-oss): The Titan goddess of the dawn. Makes things rosy with a simple touch of her fingers.

Hades (HAY-deez): Zeus's brother and the gloomy, fearsome ruler of the Underworld.

Helios (HEE-lee-us): The bright, shiny, and blinding Titan god of the sun.

Hephaestus (Hih-FESS-tuss): God of blacksmithing, metalworking, fire, volcanoes, and most things awesome.

Hera (HEER-a): Zeus's scary wife. Drives a chariot pulled by screechy peacocks.

Hestia (HESS-tee-ah): Goddess of the hearth and home. Bakes the most heavenly treats.

Persephone (per-SEFF-uh-NEE): Part-time goddess of the Underworld, part-time goddess of spring.

Poseidon (puh-SY-dun): God of the sea and controller of natural and supernatural events.

Zeus (ZOOSS): King of the gods. Fond of smiting people with lightning bolts.

OTHER MYTHICAL BEINGS

Arachne (uh-RACK-nee): Used to be a weaving woman until she ticked off the gods. Now she's a weaving spider instead.

Charon (CARE-un): The ferryman who rows the dead across the River Styx. One-way trips only.

Eurydice (yuh-RID-ih-see): Orpheus's true love. Enjoyed frolicking in the fields until she died of a snakebite.

Heracles (HAIR-a-kleez): The half-god "hero" who just loooves killing magical beasts.

Ixion (ick-SYE-on): King who pushed his father-in-law into a pit of hot coals. Now tied to a wheel in Tartarus for eternity.

Lethe (LEE-thee): Spirit of . . . something . . . can't remember . . . ah yes! The spirit of forgetfulness.

Naiads (NYE-ads): Fresh-water nymphs: keeping Olympus clean and refreshed since 500 BC.

Nymphs (NIMFS): Giggly, girly, dancing nature spirits.

Orion (uh-RY-un): A giant heroic huntsman, best known for wearing a belt made of stars.

Orpheus (OR-fee-us): A musician, a poet, and a real charmer.

Satyrs (SAY-ters): 50 percent goat, 50 percent human. 100 percent party animal.

Silenus (sy-LEE-nus): Dionysus's best friend. Old and wise, but not that good at beast-care.

PLACES

Arcadia (ar-CAY-dee-a): Wooded hills in Greece where the nymphs like to play.

Styx (STICKS): A dark river separating the Underworld from the land of the living.

Tartarus (TAR-ta-russ): A delightful torture dungeon miles below the Underworld.

BEASTS

Cerberus (SUR-ber-uss): Three-headed guard dog whose only weaknesses are sunshine and happiness.

Cretan Bull (KREE-tun): A furious, fire-breathing bull. Don't stand too close.

Griffin (GRIH-fin): Couldn't decide if it was better to be a lion or an eagle, so decided to be both.

Hydra (HY-druh): Nine-headed water serpent. Hera somehow finds this lovable.

ABOUT THE AUTHOR

Lucy Coats studied English and ancient history at Edinburgh University, then worked in children's publishing, and now writes full-time. She is a gifted children's poet and writes for all ages from two to teenage. She is widely respected for her lively retellings of myths. Her twelve-book series Greek Beasts and Heroes was published by Orion in the UK. Beasts of Olympus is her first US chapter-book series. Lucy's website is www.lucycoats.com. You can also follow her on Twitter @lucycoats.

ABOUT THE ILLUSTRATOR

As a kid, **Brett Bean** made stuff up to get out of trouble. As an adult, Brett makes stuff up to make people happy. Brett creates art for film, TV, games, books, and toys. He works on his tan and artwork in California with his wife, Julie Anne, and son, Finnegan Hobbes. He hopes to leave the world a little bit better for having him. You can find more about Brett and his artwork at www.2dbean.com.